吴健 · 著名油画家

和而不同　美而致远——

吴 健

WU JIAN

上海书画出版社

封面：
阳光下

- 美国 DORSAY 画廊
- 美国 NECCA 博物馆
- 美国 REVEL 画廊
- 中国台湾 亚洲艺术中心
- 美国 PEJMAN GALLERY
- 中国台湾 晴山艺术中心
- 中国上海大剧院画廊

图版编辑：高采霞
文字编辑：吴　帆
英文编辑：吴　帆
设　　计：颜　英
　　　　　　赵松华
摄　　影：马　军
封面题字：刘海粟

目录
CONTENTS

艺术无界。
而艺术的意义远不止于此。

不同国家、不同种族、不同语言、不同信仰，
赋予世界的精彩纷呈和开放多元，
也造成人们彼此的隔阂和错意。
尤其在众生喧哗的数字当代，
每个人都急于表达，不善倾听；
都忙于惊扰出世，无暇观照内心；
对立、冲突、争执，愤愤不平息，
成为时代的集体症候。

出路在哪里？或许并无解。
然而，在艺术的无界之中，
起码存在这样的可能——
纷繁中，一方纯净天真的天地，
桎梏中，一份心灵自由的表达，
极速中，一段曼妙优美的时光……

吴健，一位执着于绘画艺术的旅美画家，
一位游走于纽约与上海两地的文化旅者，
以他超过半个世纪的艺术创作历程，
不懈地表达这样的艺术理念与生活激情——
艺术，是通天的巴别高塔、让语言不通的人们畅意交流，
艺术，以共同的美好，将人类情感紧紧关联在一起，
艺术，是大美而无界。

和，而不同，
美，而致远，
是吴健画笔下所呈现出的美丽心灵，带给世界最深的感动，与感悟。

吴 帆
作于上海交通大学文化创意产业学院
2019 年 6 月

积厚流广说吴健

朱国荣

　　我认识吴健，已经有近三十年了。记得在20世纪70年代中后期上海的每一次画展上，几乎都能看到吴健的作品，获奖的也不在少数。他的一幅描绘瞻仰者参观中共"一大"会址的油画《党课》曾经在许多报刊杂志上发表。在我们这个年龄段的人，对这幅画至今都保留着深刻的印象。

　　1986年，吴健作为访问学者去了美国。之后，有关他的行踪时有耳闻，却看不到他的作品。这些年来，随着上海经济的高速发展，城市面貌日新月异，出国发展的上海画家便常回来看看，见面的机会多了，见画的机会也多了。吴健依然是胖胖的、笑眯眯的，几乎没变。吴健的画也依然是写实的、扎扎实实的，好像也没什么变。如果仔细回想一下，吴健的画其实变化还是很大的。

　　吴健刚到美国后，画的内容基本上是描绘中国少数民族风情和江南水乡风景。写实的画风中逐渐摆脱如实的描写，有意识地追求运笔的趣味和营造东方的意境。约从20世纪90年代起，西藏风情与花卉静物进入吴健的画面。在20世纪最后的几年里，吴健的创作视角又有了新的调整，芭蕾舞女与欧美风景画成了画面的主角。可以说，美国人的喜好从某种程序上引导了一部分中国画家的创作方向。最近当我看到吴健的油画近作时，这种感受尤为强烈。

　　吴健对芭蕾舞女这一题材的表现兴趣，可以回溯到20世纪80年代他对体育题材的创作上。当时他对自由体操女运动员的多次描绘，实际上已经启开了一个创作母题，而不是一个创作题材。虽然早在那个年代，吴健的画笔曾经触及过弹钢琴的女孩和穿芭蕾舞衣裙的女孩，但是并未有意识地作为一个母题来深入开掘。其实就在那时，吴健的心中已经有了一条涌动着创作激情的主线，即表现少女的美。恐怕当时连吴健自己也未必清楚地认识到这一点。这就是后来为什么他在画了很长一段时期的少数民族女孩子（包括藏族女孩子）之后，又会重新回到芭蕾舞女上来的原因。描绘少数民族女孩子，漂亮的服饰能够使人感到新奇，但并不能表现出处于含苞欲放青春期少女的那种特有的美。少女美，既包含着尚未发育完全的形体美，也包含了尚未成熟的童心美。正如雷维尔（Revel）画廊的艺评家迈克尔·亨利在评价吴健的画时所说："这是人体精致美妙的再现，曲线玲珑的头部、拱起背影、抬举的手臂，表现这些细部差别的能力是异乎寻常的天赋，画家抓住了形体的本质和精髓，他因此而脱颖而出。"吴健回到了芭蕾舞的少女身边，心中的爱化为创作的激情，这是艺术成功的重要条件之一。

　　说起画芭蕾舞，谁都会想到德加。德加以表现排练场和不完整的舞台演出画面为特色，或练功，或休息，或演出的舞女们总是处于一种冷漠而孤独的生活圈子中。有人说，德加主要是画色彩，这只讲对了一半。在德加的芭蕾舞画中，其实也包含了德加的思想，对舞女的深切的同情和怜悯。吴健笔下的芭蕾舞女通常也是在排练厅，她们相互交谈，和谐相处，没有孤独，没有悲哀。吴健既着意于表现舞女们优美的身姿，又力图表现出她们的纯真本质，这便是吴健不同于其他画芭蕾舞女画家的地方。吴健喜爱将芭蕾舞女置于练功房的大玻璃镜子旁，通过镜面映照来多角度地表现人物的身姿，这是吴健最拿手、最得意的看家绝活。吴健还会把双人像有意识地画成好像对镜式的奇妙效果，如《后窗》《姐妹》《背光的窗前》《舞裙》等，这一创作手法在中外古今绘画中是绝无仅有的。许多人都说，吴健运用了印象派的色彩。而我并不这样认为。我同意以下这一观点：吴健秉承并发扬了文艺复兴时期绘画大师的风格。所不同的是，吴健将光线发挥得如此淋漓尽致，以致给人以印象画的错觉。吴健是一位注重于表现光与形的写实派画家，而不是研究表现光与色的印象派画家。吴健的色彩更多地带有主观的意图，而不是客观的真实。冷色调中的舞女宁静优雅，像春水一般轻盈妩媚；暖色调中的舞女如一丛橙色的花，孕育着温暖和热烈。听说美国人很喜爱吴健的芭蕾舞作品，我想这与画面透露的快乐情调和温馨气氛有相当关系。

　　吴健的欧美风景画留给我深深的印象，尤其是画中耐人寻味的情调。这不是指画面描绘的景色，而是指笼罩于景色的散文诗般的、轻音乐般的"情调"。这词似乎有点老套了。我想说的是，在吴健的欧美风景画里，有一种与别人的画很不一样的感觉。我曾仔细欣赏和琢磨他这类作品为什么会给我有这种感觉。后来我发现，也许是那些稍稍有点模糊的笔触将清新的、带着湿度的空气奇妙地浮动在画面上。现在画画的人多用照片，很少直接写生完成。我猜想吴健也会使用照片，但是他能将照片运用得如此生动，如果没有切身的生命体验和心灵感悟，是难以表现出这似有非有的空气质感和令人神往的诗情画意的。

　　荀子曰："积厚者流泽广，积薄者流泽狭也。"根植于厚土的吴健将来在绘画风格上也许还会变，那意味着他新的起航。

（朱国荣：美术评论家、原上海市美术家协会副主席兼秘书长、中国美术家协会理事）

Inspirit and Enrich The Art of Wu Jian

By Zhu Gourong

Secretary General of the Shanghai Artists'Association

I have known Wu Jian for 30 years. In the 1970's, his paintings were often shown throughout China; and some of them had the honor of win-ning many prestigious awards of fine art. One of his most well known oil paintings,entitled"The Youth of China"was published in a range of mass media including art magazines and newspapers. This painting made an impression on a whole generation of Chinese people.

Wu Jian went to America as a visiting scholar in 1986. From then on, I seldom saw his art. With the coming era of rapid development in China, many ex-patriot artists have come back to their homeland attracted by the great opportunities currently available. Wu Jian is one of them, hav-ing recently returned for a one-man show. At first glance, he has

changed little in his appearance, and his artwork. Nevertheless, if you pay close attention to his paintings you will feel amazed in the nuance.

In his first several years in America, Wu Jian focused on painting the exotic lifestyle of minority people and the unique landscape of southern China. During the 1990's, the subject of Tibet and flowers became an important component of his paintings. But by the end of the 20th centu-ry, the ballet dancer and the landscapes of European overwhelmed all of the other topics to become the most important theme.

Wu Jian showed great interest in the beauty of girlhood during the 1980's in his paintings of young gymnasts. He was deeply inspired by the attractiveness and innocence of youth, that he couldn't help but con-vey these feelings onto canvas. These passions drove him back to the emotional theme years after as he began his series on the ballet. The inspiration from the inner and outer beauty of youth helps Wu Jian to create the elegance of nuance in his art.

Thus one won't be surprised that Michael Henry of Gallery Revel New York has said that: "No doubt Degas will be mentioned when speaking of Wu Jian's paintings of the ballet. Degas objectified the dancers while they were rehearsing. He served almost as voyeur into the world of dance. In contrast, the ballet dancers in Wu Jian's paintings are more compassionate. Wu Jian tries to pay attention to their beauty both exte-rior and interior thus making them individual and filled with their own personality. Like Degas, Wu Jian does pay close attention to the compo-sition, with special emphasis on a third reflective dimension. This is the most original and creative method of the artist, which make his painting unique from others of the same genre."

Some critics say that Wu Jian is following the colorful technique of impressionism. However, I disagree and as far as I am concerned, Wu Jian is closer to the painting style of the Renaissance. His use of light and color might lead some people to think his technique is related to impressionism. In fact Wu Jian is rather a realist painter focusing on the light and shadow. He does not persuade the objective reality about color as impressionism, but emphasizes more on the subjective reality. One can find that the peace and elegance of the dancers are somehow showing up in a cold tone, while the ardor and passion of the dancers are expressing in a warm manner.

Wu Jian's paintings of Europe also impress me. It is not the scene itself but the subtle poetic and melodious atmosphere that attracts me the most. The viewer gets the feeling of delicate and slight mood built up by the foggy but fresh environment. Without the experience and insight from real life, it is impossible to convey this is a painting.

One of the masters in ancient China said:"Enrich oneself to be great". Artist Wu Jian is one who will never stop inspiring himself with the moment of this beautiful life. We are looking forward to his next achievement. And we never doubt that it will happen.

选择芭蕾和西藏的理由

马尚龙

对于许多人来说，他可以不熟知油画的历史和流派，但是这并不妨碍他可以欣赏油画；他可以不了解芭蕾的演变和技巧，但是这并不妨碍他可以喜欢芭蕾；他可以不知道西藏的真谛和风俗，但是这并不妨碍他可以憧憬西藏。而当芭蕾、西藏以各种极其精致优雅、极其细致入微的形式，浓缩在一个画家的油画中时，从艺术的角度来看，它们必将产生出有别于它们本身、却丝毫不逊色于它们本身的魅力。这就是为什么当我翻开吴健先生的画册时，虽然我不懂画、却会被画家笔下的芭蕾舞者和西藏深深吸引的原因。源自西方宁静的芭蕾和地处中国古朴的西藏，轻盈的芭蕾和厚重的西藏、典雅的芭蕾和质拙的西藏，反差强烈地融合在吴健先生的画中。我以为，芭蕾和西藏是吴健先生画中最精华的部分。

在和吴健先生闲聊过后，我证实了我的一些猜测，证实了我对吴健先生选择芭蕾和西藏作为着力描摹对象的理由。

我猜想，吴健先生是极其欣赏和酷爱芭蕾的，这种欣赏和酷爱来自于他的青年时代。20 世纪的 50、60 年代，包括电影、戏剧、音乐在内的西方艺术，在中国几乎处于真空阶段，唯有芭蕾舞，却通过俄罗斯的芭蕾舞皇后乌兰诺娃的舞姿，广泛而深入地流传到了中国。虽然，当时很年轻的吴健先生没有选择的权力，但是，当美轮美奂的芭蕾舞绽放在苍白的年代时，吴健先生，包括他的许多同时代人，都对芭蕾怀有特别热烈的憧憬和深切的记忆，只是他的许多同时代人没有能力记载，或者忽略了记载。吴健先生却是在到了中年，以极其细腻的画笔描绘了芭蕾的魅力和美丽。于是我就想，即使在青年时期给予吴健先生选择的权力，那么按照他儒雅的性格和风度，他极有可能还是会选择芭蕾。顺便说一句，我不知道在英语中"儒雅"应该如何翻译，我觉得似乎可以用"绅士"来对应，吴健先生颇具绅士风度，一个绅士欣赏和喜欢芭蕾，是不需要理由的。

于是，芭蕾舞女就很鲜活地舞蹈在吴健先生的画布中。我不禁赞叹吴健先生的细腻，所有的场景都是在芭蕾舞女的练功房里，几乎就是芭蕾舞女美景的链接。看着这样的画，我想像着吴健先生的角色，他距离芭蕾女非常近，却不在练功房里，因为她们静谧，怡然，超凡，完全沉浸在芭蕾舞飘飘欲仙的境界里，根本就察觉不到一个旁观者的所在——吴健先生仿佛就在窗外张望着她们，充满着对美的憧憬和对艺术的感悟。

后来吴健先生告诉我，他喜欢芭蕾舞，乃至他的这一组芭蕾舞女的画，确实来自于几十年前乌兰诺娃在中国演出的芭蕾舞。

那么西藏呢？藏民的场景，无疑是吴健先生画中另一个重要的组合。它与芭蕾舞女迥然不同，如果说"芭蕾舞"像是小提琴的悠扬婉转，那么"西藏"就几乎是大提琴的深沉浑厚，强烈地显示出吴健先生风格的多样。我猜想，吴健先生就像酷爱芭蕾一样地爱着西藏特有的神秘、古朴和圣洁；我猜测，他就像那么接近于芭蕾舞女一样接近过西藏。确实，吴健先生在 20 世纪 90 年代曾经两次去西藏，创作出一组令西方观众耳目一新的画作。我曾经去过藏民生活的地区，在看了吴健先生画笔下的西藏后，我为自己而遗憾，因为我的视线所及，就显得非常的狭窄。但是因为我曾经去过，所以，我简直就能从吴健先生的画中，闻到西藏的酥油茶和青稞酒。好多年以来，西藏作为一个文化符号，吸引着世界，吴健先生恰似西藏文化的一个传播者。他画笔下的西藏，不是浮光掠影，不是走马观花，而是显示出了西藏的文化个性，所以我觉得，吴健先生是一个用画笔写作的作家，或者说他是一个饱含着文化思考的画家。有多少人爱西藏却因为恐惧高原反应而退避，但是吴健先生勇敢地去了，还去了两次，终于成就了这一组非凡的作品。

吴健先生的画当然不止于芭蕾和西藏，比如还有中国江南水乡和异国的风景等等，这其中有更多纯艺术的境界，使我这个不懂画的人无法描述。但是有一点是显然的，那便是欣赏着吴健先生的画，我的心情便非常旷达、安宁和愉悦，时不时地产生会意和共鸣。我想，对于大多数观众来说，这就足够了。

Inspirit and Enrich The Art of Wu Jian

Ma Shanglong

You may enjoy oil paintings before you know its history and genre. You may like ballet without knowing its evolvement and skills. You may long for Tibet even if you have no idea about its customs and tradition. But when an artist, in delicate and elegant forms, brings ballet and Tibet forward to you on the canvas, the appearance will be different from themselves, but not less fascinating than themselves. That's the reason why I was deeply moved by the ballet and the Tibet in the paintings of Mr. Wu Jian. The lightness and elegance of western originated ballet, and the massiveness and simplicity of eastern located Tibet, are permeated in Mr. Wu Jian's paintings. In my opinion, ballet and Tibet constitute the essence of Mr. Wu Jian's works.

Mr. Wu Jian got to know ballet in his youth and then fell deeply impressed. In the 50s and 60s of the last century, all western culture including movies, opera and music were blocked from Mainland China, except ballet. Ballet was well introduced to Chinese people by Ulanova, the Russian Queen of Ballet. Young Wu Jian had no other choices, but he, as well as many of his coevals, was so touched by the splendid performance of ballet that deep impression remained. His Peers may have ignored the memory of ballet, but Mr. Wu Jian recalled and depicted the good memory of fascinating and beautiful ballet when he was middle aged. I imagine, if young Wu Jian was able to choose, he would sill have chosen ballet, by his cultured and gentle character. Mr. Wu Jian loves ballet in the way a gentleman does.

Then what about Tibet. Life in Tibet is another part of Mr. Wu Jian's paintings, in contrast to the paintings of ballerinas. If ballet is described as sweet and melodious as a violin, then Tibet is as deep and vigorous as acello. These paintings show the diversity of Mr. Wu Jian's style. I assume Mr. Wu Jian loves the mysterious primitive Tibet just as he loves ballet. I assume Mr. Wu Jian has been as close to Tibetans as he has been to ballerinas. In fact, Mr. Wu Jian visited Tibet twice in the 1990s and then produced a session of paintings that were refreshing to westerners. I feel pity that I didn't have such broad view when I visited Tibet, but my experience makes me understand Mr. Wu Jian's paintings better - I can even smell the ghee tea and the highland barley wine of Tibet. Tibet has long been a symbol of eastern culture, attractive to the outer world. Mr. Wu Jian is a disseminator of Tibetan culture. His paintings about Tibet, are neither skimming over the surface, nor superficial understanding through cursory observation, but reveal the connotation of Tibetan culture. Mr. Wu Jian is a writer, writing with his painting brush. Mr. Wu Jian is a painter, painting with thoughts of culture. Many Tibet lovers retreat in fears of altitude sickness, but Mr. Wu Jian took the adventure bravely and went there twice. This group of masterpieces is a produce of his braveness.

Mr. Wu Jian depicts more than ballet and Tibet. For instance, he paints about watery regions in southeast China and the landscape of the western countryside. The essence of pure art may be too difficult for me to tell, but I enjoy peacefulness and joviality in Mr. Wu Jian's paintings, according to my own understanding. Joy is the most important feeling for most art lovers.

主 题 创 作

THEME AUTHORING

党课（局部） 1971 年

学生运动草图　1985 年

学生运动　1986 年

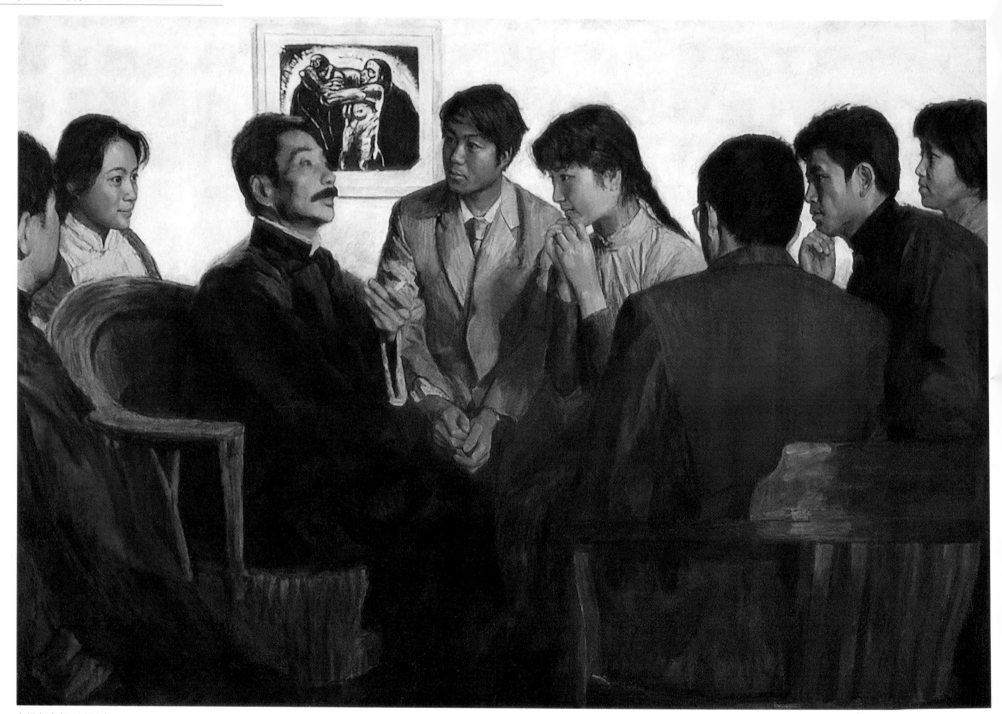

鲁迅与青年 1984 年

图书馆　1985 年

归 1984 年

丝路　1984 年

休息　1982 年

司机　1984 年

海南岛孩子　1984 年

骑手　1984 年

芭蕾教室　1984 年

国家队员 1985 年

体操运动员　1984 年

锻炼身体为国争光 DUAN LIAN SHEN TI WEI GUO ZHENG GUANG

wei da de zuguo zai zhao huan

伟大的祖国在召唤

宣传画 5 幅

宣传画 1984 年

宣传画 1983 年

加强纪律性 革命无不胜

友爱同学

YOUAITONGXUE

教育必须为无产阶级政治服务
教育必须同生产劳动相结合

宣传画 4幅

宣传画 4 幅

与赵渭凉合

刘胡兰宣传画

独幅版画

现代剧：
红色娘子军

现代剧：
海港

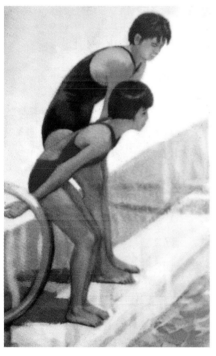

扭扭秧花是民兵连长，
正举起望远镜（jìng），向海面
了望。
海水起伏翻滚，溅起的
浪花，在阳光下闪闪发光。
扭扭秧心想着，眼前，看出来
花里面有一点特别明亮的光
点，在慢慢的前移（yí）动。

儿童插页 8 幅

连环画

油 画

OIL PAINTING

对影　2000 年

沉思　2002 年

背光 1999 年

排练室 2001 年

镜前 1995 年

黑色舞裙　2015 年

窗前的花　2000 年

汉娜　2015 年

德国女孩　1999 年

婷立　2008 年

后窗　2014 年

休息　2003 年

中国女孩　2004 年

琴边　2003 年

后台　1999 年

白色的扇子　2006 年

长舞裙　2004 年

坐着的萨拉   2002 年

黑色舞裙　2012 年

窗台　1998 年

萨拉 1998 年

纱裙　1988 年

侧光　1987 年

舞裙 2001 年

粉色舞裙　2012 年

汉娜　2011 年

拿花的萨拉　2005 年

白色舞裙 2015 年

友情　2014 年

红墙 2013 年

穿黄衣的女孩们　2014 年

舞蹈课 1999 年

镜前的芭蕾女孩们　2014 年

两个女孩　1999 年

长岛舞蹈学校　2002 年

百老汇舞校   2011 年

芭蕾女孩们　2011 年

五彩舞裙　2000 年

在后台的舞校学生　2001 年　　　　　　　　　　　　　　　　　　　　NY 舞蹈学校　1999 年

黑与白　2010 年

汉娜与朋友　2009 年

谈心　2010 年

背光的窗前　2011 年

黄色的舞裙 2010 年

红窗　2013 年

兰衣芭蕾女孩　2010 年

窗前 1999 年

长岛舞校 2002 年

NY 57 街舞校　2010 年

后台　1998 年

等待排练 2013 年

排练前 2013 年

红窗 2014 年

阳光 2015 年

后台 2018 年

集市 2005 年

窗下　2017 年

阳光下　2015 年

夫妇 2000 年

路边 2000 年

藏族女孩们   2014 年

藏族新娘　2016 年

阳光下　1989 年

土墙 1989 年

背光的女孩们　1990 年

盛装 2013 年

挑水 1990 年

草原 2013 年

大树下　2001 年

行走　2011 年

美丽的藏女　2014 年

牵牛的人 1990 年

新娘 2016 年

水边　2005 年

阳光 2001 年

小溪　1994 年

新疆女孩 1987 年

别离　2010 年

野餐 1988 年

回家路上 1988 年

小憩 1985 年

帐篷内 1988 年

母与子 1990 年

藏女与马　1988 年

冬日阳光　2009 年

海南女孩　1985 年

集市　2011 年

云南母与子　2000 年

女子　2016 年

布拉格女孩　2002 年

自画像

盛装　2017 年

中央公园　2010 年

红花　2010 年

小花 2005 年

华丽的静物 2000 年

红玫瑰　2001 年

金色　2000 年

玛莎家的花　1988 年

花　1987 年

银器　1988 年

花与钟　2000 年

背光　2016 年

绿色镜子　2011 年

鱼 1982 年

面包 1983 年

夜色　1999 年

铁桥　2011 年

巴黎的桥　1999 年

日内瓦　2001 年

巴黎纪念碑　2000 年

傍晚　2011 年

河边的教堂　2001 年

威尼斯小桥 2011 年

海上　2002 年

芬兰海边　2010 年

塞纳河畔　1988 年

英国乡间　2000 年

瑞士 2001 年

中央公园 1990 年

雪 1989 年

纽约的秋天 2011 年

藏区 1982 年

倒影 2000 年

周庄秋色 1989 年

水乡 1990 年

桥 1985 年

速 写

SKETCH

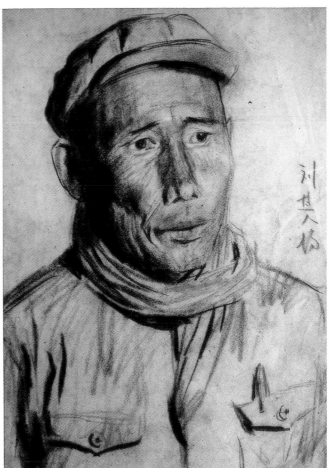

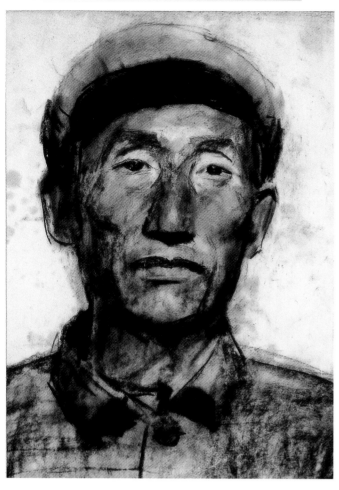

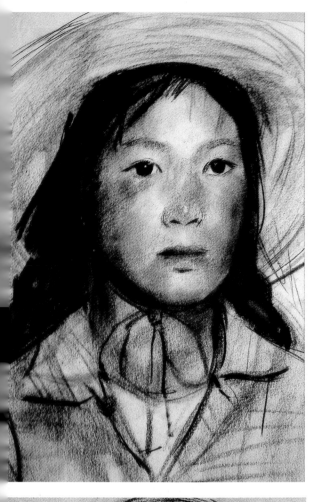

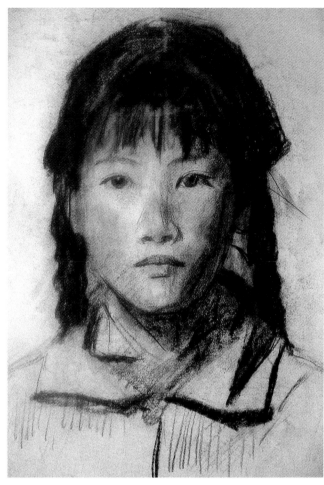

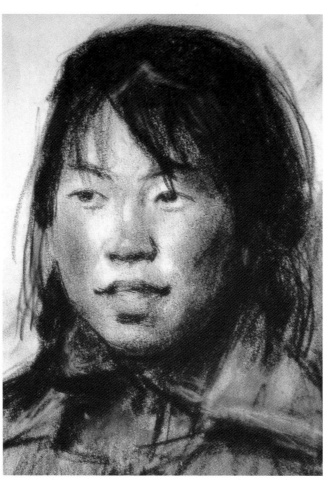

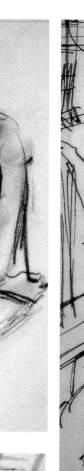

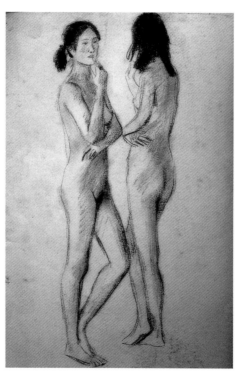

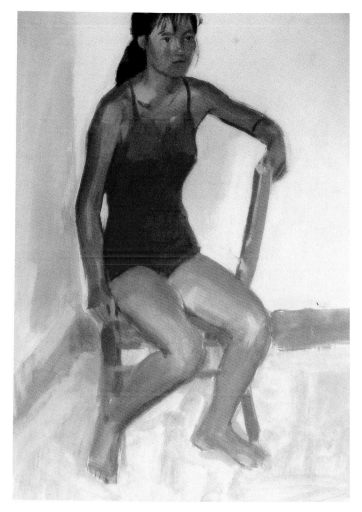

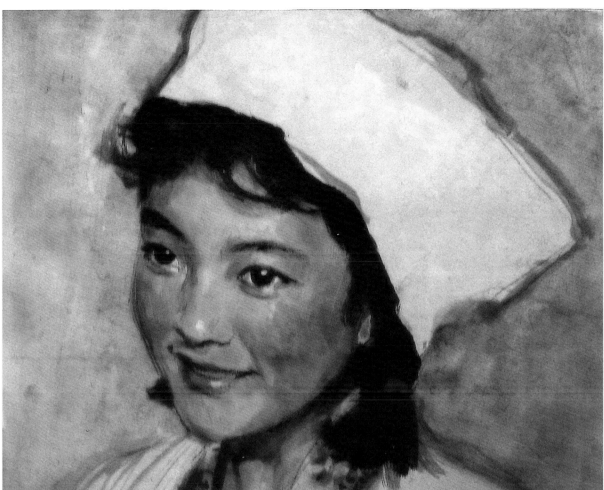

外滩　1982 年

市中心　1982 年

四川北路桥　1981 年

街道　1982 年

金色乡间 1981年

小镇 1981年

乡间 1981年

风景 4 幅 1981 年

傍晚　1982 年

船边　1984 年

船　1983 年

太湖　1985 年

银色　1982 年

船　1981 年

渔轮 3 幅 1982 年

靠岸　1982 年

沈家门　1982 年

水乡　1982 年

湖南乡间　1982 年

乡间 1981 年

乡间 1981 年

桥 1981 年

早期作品

EARLY WORKS

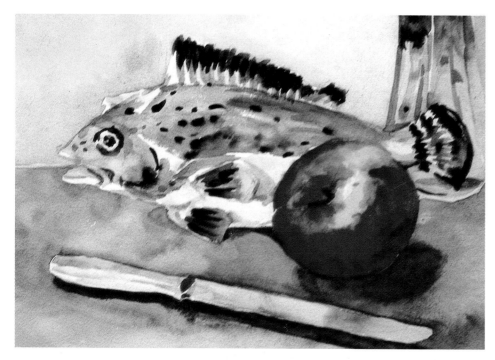

对面的屋顶　1960 年

屋顶 1959 年

街道 1960 年

175

房子 1981 年

城门 1982 年

秋色 1981 年

屋 1978 年

船 1961 年

船上　1980 年

女学生 1985 年

小提琴手 1985 年

运动员　1982 年

花布女孩　　1984 年

农场女孩　1982 年

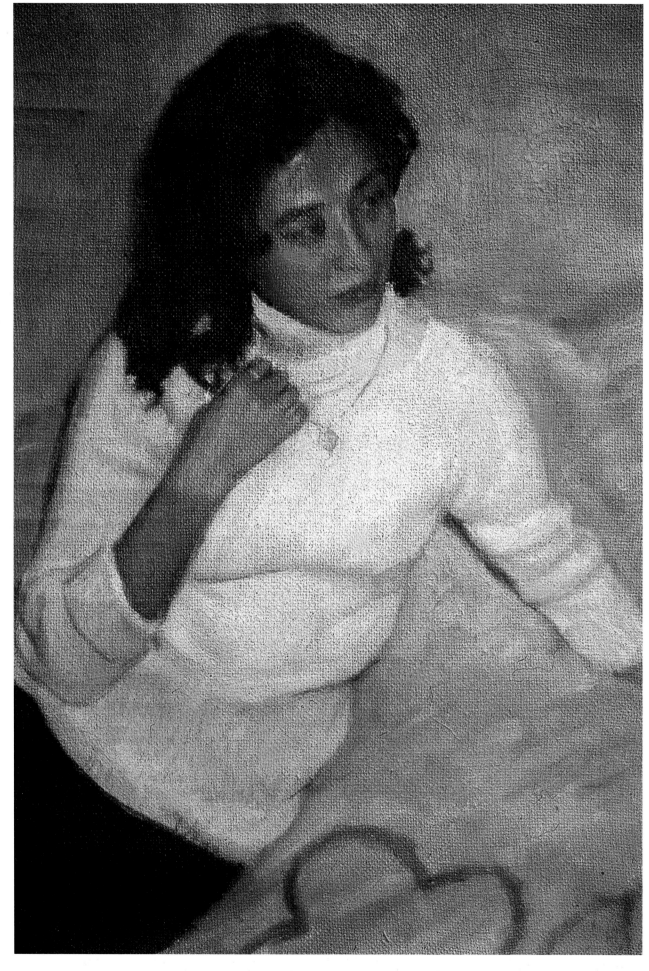

妻子　1982 年

妻子与猫 1985 年

女儿 1985 年

大提琴手 1985 年

长发姑娘 1985 年

自画像 1980 年

拿扇女 1985 年

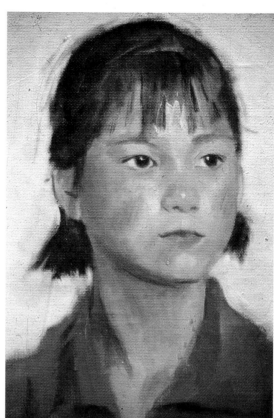

女孩 1981 年

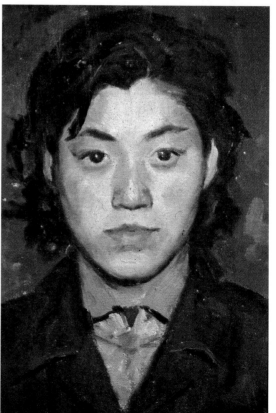

女子头像 1983 年

女民警　1982 年

白衣女　1985 年

粉丝　1986 年

海南女　1985 年

读信　1985 年

绿色毛衣　1985 年

185

舞房 1986 年

人体 1984 年

人体 1984 年

女孩　1984 年

女孩　1985 年

女孩　1986 年

渔娘 1982 年

赛前 1999 年

女孩 1984 年

拿花女孩　1989 年

肖像 1995 年

费兰　1989 年

弹吉他女孩 1986 年

肖像 1997 年

肖像　1998 年

人像 1997 年

人像 1997 年

云南女孩　2000 年

肖像 2000 年

云南女孩 2000 年

藏族妇女　1988 年　　　　　　　　　　　　　　　　　　　凝视　1985 年

海南妇女　1985 年

云南女孩　1985 年　　　　　　　　　　　　　　　　　　　　族姑娘　1984 年

藏男 1984 年

藏女 1985 年

新疆女孩　1982 年

藏女　1987 年

少数民族　1987 年

个人资料

PERSONAL INFORMATION

摄于大峡谷　1989 年

摄于刘海粟美术馆前

在家中

摄于西安　1985 年

父母送我出国　1986 年　　　　　　　　　女儿　　　　　　　　女儿

写生　1985 年　　　　　摄于藏区　1985 年　　　　　临摹法国油画　1985 年　　　　　在创作

与交通大学校长合影（右二） 1985 年

刘海粟与

刘海粟与王

与俞云阶老师（左二）

与陈逸飞

在陈逸飞的画室，陈逸飞在创作《踱步》

与陈逸飞

与朋友合影（前左三为陈逸飞）

摄于长岛画廊 1988 年

与陈逸飞在吴健个展上合影 1987 年

与英国、法国、德国大学校长合影 1984 年

在画廊 1997 年

吴健夫妇与美国收藏家 1986 年

上海大剧院个展合影

吴健夫妇与收藏家 1986 年

记者采访

在交通大学的画展上合影（左二为马尚龙，右五是戴敦邦，右四是黄英浩）

2016 年 10 月，交通大学校庆 120 周年之际，吴健《远涉归来》画展在上海交大程及美术馆举办

吴健于 1942 年出生于中国浙江省，从小就对艺术产生浓厚的兴趣。他熟练掌握了透视、构图、造型等传统技法，很快就获得了外界的关注，随着吴健绘画技艺的成熟，因为他的杰出的才华被邀请参加多个全国性展览，并获得了中国美术家协会会员的殊荣。

　　20 世纪 80 年代吴健移民到美国后，他在旧金山美术学院和纽约艺术学生联盟继续深造，很快就受到了纽约艺术界的广泛欢迎，并于 1988 年在新英格兰当代艺术中心举办了他在美国的首次个人画展。

　　吴健曾多次参加遍布美国和其他国家和地区的众多展览，牢固建立了自己绘画艺术大师的形象，作品陈列在中国美术馆以及世界各地的美术馆，也有众多私人和公共的收藏。

　　吴健的绘画将他在现实主义本质与对光影的深刻研究结合起来，并从印象派中汲取灵感。正如缅因州艺术学院甘旭博士所宣称的那样，"看到吴健芭蕾舞女演员的画作，很自然地就联想到法国印象派画家德加作品中所展示的美丽"。

　　无论是以年轻芭蕾舞演员的纯真为特色的作品，还是以静谧的风景为特色的作品，吴健凭借独特的视野和高超的技巧捕捉到了每一刻的凄美。他专注于细节的能力使观众的想象突破画作的局限，这些都使吴健在艺术家群体中脱颖而出。每个笔触都体现了厚度、色彩和质感，同时捕捉了绘画对象的内在美与外在美。

　　曾经有人这样说："充实自己，让自己更伟大。"艺术家吴健是一个永远会激励自己达到更高水平的绘画大师。

多尔赛画廊

Born in the Zheijang Province of China in 1942, Wu Jian took an interest in art at an early age. Mastering the traditional techniques of perspective, composition and form, he quickly achieved notice and was invited to study at the prestigious Academy of Fine Arts in Shanghai. As Jian matured, his exceptional talent garnered invitations into several national juried exhibitions and earned him the distinction of serving as a member of the National Association of Fine Art in China.

After immigrating to the United States in the 1980's, Jian further pursued his studies at the San Francisco Academy of Fine Art and the Art Student's League of New York. Promptly welcomed into the New York art world, Wu Jian received much acclaim and was awarded his first solo museum show in America at the New England Center of Contemporary Art in 1988.

Now in his seventies, Wu Jian has participated in numerous exhibitions throughout the United States as well as abroad, firmly establishing himself as a master painter, with works hanging in the China National Art Museum as well as private and public collections throughout the world.

Wu's painting combines his roots in realism with a profound study of light and shadow that takes inspiration from the Impressionists. As proclaimed by Dr. Gan Xu of the Maine College of Art"One can hardly look at paintings of Wu Jian's ballerinas without association of French Impressionist Degas".

Whether it is his compositions featuring the innocence of young ballerinas or the serenity of a landscape, Jian's well-trained eye and superb technique captures the poignant beauty in each moment. His ability to focus on subtle events enables the viewer to transcend the physical boundaries of the image captured, and has set Jian apart from his peers. Each brushstroke embodies volume, color and texture, capturing both the inner and outer beauty of his subject.

One of the masters in ancient China said:"Enrich oneself to be great." Artist Wu Jian is one who will never stop inspiring himself to achieve greater levels of masterful painting.

Galerie Dorsay

艺术简历

陈逸飞画作者

博物馆展览

美国康乃狄克州，NECCA 博物馆

美国俄亥俄州，Spring field 美术馆

美国佛罗里达州，Houywood 艺术文化中心

美国麻州，American International college，Garret 画廊

美国德州，Michelson Reves 美术馆

美国宾州，Washington & Jefferson College 艺术画廊

美国田纳西州，University of Tennessee 艺术画廊

美国佛蒙州，Brattleboro 博物馆

美国威斯康辛州，Leigh yawkey wood son 美术馆

拍卖记录

1992 年 –2000 年

佳士德 (HK)

佳士德 (HK) 中国当代油画

苏富比 (HK) 中国当代油画

新加坡中国艺术品拍卖

中国台湾标竿艺术

中国台湾儒家艺术精品拍卖会

中国嘉德国际拍卖有限公司

美国加州 Clark Cierlak Fine Art

目前作品已被美国 NECCA 博物馆、上海美术馆、上海鲁迅纪念馆香港徐氏博物馆等典藏，于私人收藏部分，更遍及美国、英国、日本、俄罗斯和中国台湾地区等地

辞条被辑入：《北美美术家名人》《中国当代美术家人名》《中国美术辞海》《北美华裔艺术家名人》

Inspirit and Enrich The Art of Wu Jian

MUSEUM SHOWS

NECCA Museum, BrookLyn. Connecticutt

Springfield Art Museum, Springfield, Ohio

Hollywood Art & Culture Center, Hollywood, Florida

American International College, Garret Gallery, Massachusetts

Michelson Reves Museum of Art, Marshall, Texas

Washington & Jefferson College Art Gallery, Washington, Pennsylvania

University of Tennessee Art Gallery, Knoxville, Tennessee

Brattleboro Museum, Brattleboro, Vermont

Leigh Yawkey Woodsom Art Museum, Wausau, Wisconsin

Auction Record

(1992-2000)

Christies'-HK

Christies'-HK

Sothehy's -HK

Associate Fine Art Auctionees-Singapare

Concarde Fine Art Auctionees-Taipei, China

Heritage Art International LTD-Taipei, China

China Guardian Auction Co.LTD-Beijing

Clark Cierlak Fine Art-CA.USA

MUSEUM COLLECTIONS

LuXun Museum-Shanghai China Museum NECCA US

Tsui Museum of Art, Hong Kong

Shanghai Fine Art Museum China

图书在版编目 (CIP) 数据

和而不同　美而致远：吴健／吴帆，高采霞编 .-- 上海：
上海书画出版社 ,2019.9
ISBN 978-7-5479-2190-6

Ⅰ . ①和… Ⅱ . ①吴… ②高… Ⅲ . ①油画 - 作品集
- 中国 - 现代 Ⅳ . ① J223.8

中国版本图书馆 CIP 数据核字 (2019) 第 216652 号

和而不同　美而致远——吴健

吴 帆　高采霞　编

统　筹	吴迪
责任编辑	苏 醒
审　读	雍琦
技术编辑	包赛明

出版发行	上海世纪出版集团 上海书画出版社
地址	上海市延安西路593号　200050
网址	www.ewen.co www.shshuhua.com
E-mail	shcpph@163.com
印刷	上海界龙艺术印刷有限公司
经销	各地新华书店
开本	889×1194　1/12
印张	18
版次	2019年10月第1版　2019年10月第1次印刷
印数	1000
书号	ISBN 978-7-5479-2190-6
定价	280.00元

若有印刷、装订质量问题，请与承印厂联系

丹青品格　怡養我心

敬請關注上海書畫出版社